THE
BANJO MAN

Ben Paviour Short - his book

First published by Ashton Scholastic Ltd, 1990
This paperback edition published 1991

Ashton Scholastic Limited
Private Bag 1, Penrose, Auckland 5, New Zealand.

Ashton Scholastic Pty Ltd
P.O. Box 579, Gosford, NSW 2250, Australia.

Scholastic Inc.
730 Broadway, New York, NY 10003, USA.

Scholastic Canada Ltd
123 Newkirk Road, Richmond Hill, Ontario L4C 3G5, Canada.

Scholastic Publications Ltd
Villiers House, Clarendon Avenue, Leamington Spa, Warwickshire CV32 5PR, England.

National Library of New Zealand
Cataloguing-in-Publication data

Bacon, Ron, 1924-
   The banjo man / by Ron Bacon ; illustrated by Kelvin Hawley. Auckland, N.Z. : Ashton Scholastic, 1990.
   1 v.
   Poem for children.
   For 5-7 year olds -- School Library Service, Wellington, N.Z.
   Summary: What will the banjo man conjure up when he stops his truck and starts to play the banjo.
   ISBN 1-86943-105-7
   I. Hawley, Kelvin. II. Title.
      NZ821.2

87654321   123456789/9

Designed by Julie Roil
Typesetting by Rennies Illustrations Ltd
Printed in Hong Kong

THE
BANJO MAN

BY
Ron Bacon

ILLUSTRATED BY
Kelvin Hawley

Ashton Scholastic
Auckland   Sydney   New York   Toronto   London

Autumn, when leaves are turning gold and brown.
Hear the banjo man!
Hear him coming over the hill and down the road.
Nearer — nearer!

His engine rattles over the bridge . . .
his pots, his pans, his bucket, his bath
and his bicycle too, all rattling.
His house comes down the road,
a great, grey, dusty, rattling cloud.

He stops and the dust settles.
He sits on the steps of his house
and he tightens the strings of his banjo.

Wait and hear what his banjo will say.
Watch.
Listen for the first notes he will play.

His fingers twitch a little,
they touch the strings,
then from his banjo the music comes.

Oh, those fingers on that banjo!

Sometimes they wander over the strings,
so soft, so dreamy slow,
the music is sleepy bird-talk
from night-shrouded trees.

Sometimes they tiptoe on the strings —
kittens on grass after rain.

Sometimes they come down hard on the strings
and the sound is thunder
bursting from dark, drifting skies.

Sometimes they bounce about on that banjo
so butterflies dance — dizzy — round daisies.

Or they pluck at the strings of his banjo
so ice-laden trees tinkle their twigs
when snowy winds blow through,
and slow drips slide from icicle tips
and plink into pools below.

Or hags and harridans frolic and dance
in the dark of a cloud-cloaked moon,
and peg-leg pirates hop about
— in and out —
and jig to those jangling strings.

Oh, what wonders there are in that banjo!

And when night has come, hear the sound of the banjo
still singing and ringing in all the dark air around.
Dream dreams of music and magic,
of fingers dancing, of icicles tinkling, of peg-leg pirates . . .
butterflies and daisies . . . kittens . . .
and blue-black, thunder-bursting skies.

22

Morning, and the banjo man has gone —
over some other hill, down some other road,
across some other bridge . . .

Until next autumn,
when leaves are turning gold and brown,
he comes again — the banjo man!

About the Author:

Author of more than thirty children's books, Ron Bacon is one of New Zealand's most successful and prolific writers. A former primary school principal, he now writes full time.

About the Illustrator:

New Zealander Kelvin Hawley, a former art director, has been illustrating children's books full time for the past five years, and has completed more than fifty titles to date. He currently resides in Queensland with his wife and three children.